This time, O'Reilly did the search.

The other corpse, the heavier of the two, also smelled faintly of perfume. This man had kept his wallet in the inner pocket of his suit coat, just like his companion had.

O'Reilly opened the wallet. Another badge, just like he expected. But he didn't expect the bulldog face glaring at him from the wallet's interior.

Nor had he expected the name.

"Jesus, Mary and Joseph," he said.

"What've we got?" McKinnon asked.

O'Reilly handed him the wallet, opened to the slim paper identification.

"The Director of the FBI," he said, his voice shaking. "Public Hero Number One. J. Edgar Hoover."

ALSO BY
KRISTINE KATHRYN RUSCH

THE DIVING SERIES

Diving into the Wreck: A Diving Novel

City of Ruins: A Diving Novel

Becalmed: A Diving Universe Novella

The Application of Hope: A Diving Universe Novella

Boneyards: A Diving Novel

Skirmishes: A Diving Novel

The Runabout: A Diving Novel

The Falls: A Diving Universe Novel

Searching for the Fleet: A Diving Novel

The Spires of Denon: A Diving Universe Novella

The Renegat: A Diving Universe Novel

Escaping Amnthra: A Diving Universe Novella

The Court-Martial of the Renegat Renegades

Thieves: A Diving Novel

Squishy's Teams: A Diving Universe Novel

The Chase: A Diving Novel

Maelstrom: A Diving Universe Novella

THE RETRIEVAL ARTIST SERIES

The Disappeared

Extremes

Consequences

Buried Deep

Paloma

Recovery Man

The Recovery Man's Bargain

Duplicate Effort

The Possession of Paavo Deshin

Anniversary Day

Blowback

A Murder of Clones

Search & Recovery

The Peyti Crisis

Vigilantes

Starbase Human

Masterminds

The Impossibles

The Retrieval Artist

THE FEY SERIES

The Original books of The Fey

The Sacrifice: Book One of the Fey

The Changeling: Book Two of the Fey

The Rival: Book Three of the Fey

The Resistance: Book Four of the Fey

Victory: Book Five of the Fey

The Black Throne

The Black Queen: Book One of the Black Throne

The Black King: Book Two of the Black Throne

The Qavnerian Protectorate

The Reflection on Mount Vitaki: Prequel to the Qavnerian Protectorate

The Kirilli Matter: The First Book of the Qavnerian Protectorate

Barkson's Journey: The Second Book of the Qavnerian Protectorate

Incident at Serebro Academy: The Third Book of the Qavnerian Protectorate

(coming 2024)

Writing as Kris Nelscott

THE SMOKEY DALTON SERIES

A Dangerous Road

Smoke-Filled Rooms

Thin Walls

Stone Cribs

War at Home

Days of Rage

Street Justice

AND

Protectors

———

Writing as Kristine Grayson

The Charming Trilogy, Vol. 1

The Charming Trilogy, Vol. 2

The Fates Trilogy

The Daughters of Zeus Trilogy

G-MEN

KRISTINE KATHRYN RUSCH

WMG
PUBLISHING

G-MEN

G-MEN

"There's something addicting about a secret."

~ J. Edgar Hoover

The squalid little alley smelled of piss. Detective Seamus O'Reilly tugged his overcoat closed and wished he'd worn boots. He could feel the chill of his metal flashlight through the worn glove on his right hand.

Two beat cops stood in front of the bodies, and the coroner crouched over them. His assistant was already setting up the gurneys, body bags draped over his arm. The coroner's van had blocked the alley's entrance, only a few yards away.

O'Reilly's partner, Joseph McKinnon, followed him.

McKinnon had trained his own flashlight on the fire escapes above, unintentionally alerting any residents to the police presence.

But they probably already knew. Shootings in this part of the city were common. The neighborhood teetered between swank and corrupt. Far enough from Central Park for degenerates and muggers to use the alleys as corridors, and, conversely, close enough for new money to want to live with a peak of the city's most famous expanse of green.

The coroner, Thomas Brunner, had set up two expensive, battery-operated lights on garbage can lids placed on top of the dirty ice, one at the top of the bodies, the other near the feet. O'Reilly crouched so he wouldn't create any more shadows.

"What've we got?" he asked.

"Dunno yet." Brunner was using his gloved hands to part the hair on the back of the nearest corpse's skull. "It could be one of those nights."

O'Reilly had worked with Brunner for eighteen years now, since they both got back from the war, and he hated it when Brunner said it could be one of those nights. That meant the corpses would stack up, which was usually a summer thing, but almost never happened in the middle of winter.

"Why?" O'Reilly asked. "What else we got?"

"Some colored limo driver shot two blocks from here." Brunner was still parting the hair. It took O'Reilly a minute to realize it was matted with blood. "And two white guys pulled out of their cars and shot about four blocks from that."

O'Reilly felt a shiver run through him that had nothing to do with the cold. "You think the shootings are related?"

"Dunno," Brunner said. "But I think it's odd, don't you? Five dead in the space of an hour, all in a six-block radius."

O'Reilly closed his eyes for a moment. Two white guys pulled out of their cars, one Negro driver of a limo, and now two white guys in an alley. Maybe they were related, maybe they weren't.

He opened his eyes, then wished he hadn't. Brunner had his finger inside a bullet hole, a quick way to judge caliber.

"Same type of bullet," Brunner said.

"You handled the other shootings?"

"I was on scene with the driver when some fag called this one in."

O'Reilly looked at Brunner. Eighteen years, and he still wasn't used to the man's casual bigotry.

"How did you know the guy was queer?" O'Reilly asked. "You talk to him?"

"Didn't have to." Brunner nodded toward the building in front of them. "Weekly party for degenerates in the penthouse apartment every Thursday night. Thought you knew."

O'Reilly looked up. Now he understood why McKinnon

had been shining his flashlight at the upper story windows. McKinnon had worked vice before he got promoted to homicide.

"Why would I know?" O'Reilly said.

McKinnon was the one who answered. "Because of the standing orders."

"I'm not playing twenty questions," O'Reilly said. "I don't know about a party in this building and I don't know about standing orders."

"The standing orders are," McKinnon said as if he were an elementary school teacher, "not to bust it, no matter what kind of lead you got. You see someone go in, you forget about it. You see someone come out, you avert your eyes. You complain, you get moved to a different shift, maybe a different precinct."

"Jesus." O'Reilly was too far below to see if there was any movement against the glass in the penthouse suite. But whoever lived there—whoever partied there—had learned to shut off the lights before the cops arrived.

"Shot in the back of the head," Brunner said before O'Reilly could process all of the information. "That's just damn strange."

O'Reilly looked at the corpses—really looked at them—for the first time. Two men, both rather heavy set. Their faces were gone, probably splattered all over the walls. Gloved hands, nice shoes, one of them wearing a white scarf that caught the light.

Brunner had to search for the wound in the back of the head, which made that the entry point. The exit wounds had destroyed the faces.

O'Reilly looked behind him. No door on that building, but there was one on the building where the party was held. If they'd been exiting the building and were surprised by a queer basher or a mugger, they'd've been shot in the front, not the back.

"How many times were they shot?" O'Reilly asked.

"Looks like just the once. Large caliber, close range. I'd say it was a purposeful headshot, designed to do maximum damage." Brunner felt the back of the closest corpse. "There doesn't seem to be anything on the torso."

"They still got their wallets?" McKinnon asked.

"Haven't checked yet." Brunner reached into the back pants pocket of the corpse he'd been searching and clearly found nothing. So he grabbed the front of the overcoat and reached inside.

He removed a long thin wallet—old fashioned, the kind made for the larger bills of forty years before. Hand-tailored, beautifully made.

These men weren't hurting for money.

Brunner handed the wallet to O'Reilly, who opened it. And stopped when he saw the badge inside. His mouth went dry.

"We got a feebee," he said, his voice sounding strangled.

"What?" McKinnon asked.

"FBI," Brunner said dryly. McKinnon had only moved to homicide the year before. Vice rarely had to deal with FBI. Homicide did only on sensational cases. O'Reilly could count on one hand the number of times he'd spoken to agents in the New York bureau.

"Not just any feebee either," O'Reilly said. "The Associate Director. Clyde A. Tolson."

McKinnon whistled. "Who's the other guy?"

This time, O'Reilly did the search. The other corpse, the heavier of the two, also smelled faintly of perfume. This man had kept his wallet in the inner pocket of his suit coat, just like his companion had.

O'Reilly opened the wallet. Another badge, just like he expected. But he didn't expect the bulldog face glaring at him from the wallet's interior.

Nor had he expected the name.

"Jesus, Mary and Joseph," he said.

"What've we got?" McKinnon asked.

O'Reilly handed him the wallet, opened to the slim paper identification.

"The Director of the FBI," he said, his voice shaking. "Public Hero Number One. J. Edgar Hoover."

———

Francis Xavier Bryce—Frank to his friends, what few of them he still had left—had just dropped off to sleep when the phone rang. He cursed, caught himself, apologized to Mary, and then remembered she wasn't there.

The phone rang again and he fumbled for the light, knocking over the highball glass he'd used to mix his mom's recipe for sleepless nights, hot milk, butter and honey. It turned out that, at the tender age of 36, hot milk and butter laced with honey wasn't a recipe for sleep; it was a recipe for heartburn.

And for a smelly carpet if he didn't clean the mess up.

He found the phone before he found the light.

"What?" he snapped.

"You live near Central Park, right?" A voice he didn't recognize, but one that was clearly official, asked the question without a hello or an introduction.

"More or less." Bryce rarely talked about his apartment. His parents had left it to him and, as his wife was fond of sniping, it was too fancy for a junior G-Man.

The voice rattled off an address. "How far is that from you?"

"About five minutes." If he didn't clean up the mess on the floor. If he spent thirty seconds pulling on the clothes he'd piled onto the chair beside the bed.

"Get there. Now. We got a situation."

"What about my partner?" Bryce's partner lived in Queens.

"You'll have back-up. You just have to get to the scene. The moment you get there, you shut it down."

"Um." Bryce hated sounding uncertain, but he had no choice. "First, sir, I need to know who I'm talking to. Then I need to know what I'll find."

"You'll find a double homicide. And you're talking to Eugene Hart, the Special Agent in Charge. I shouldn't have to identify myself to you."

Now that he had, Bryce recognized Hart's voice. "Sorry, sir. It's just procedure."

"Fuck procedure. Take over that scene. *Now*."

"Yes, sir," Bryce said, but he was talking into an empty phone line. He hung up, hands shaking, wishing he had some BromoSeltzer.

He'd just come off a long, messy investigation of another agent. Walter Cain had been about to get married when he remembered he had to inform the Bureau of that fact and, as per regulation, get his bride vetted before walking down the aisle.

Bryce had been the one to investigate the future Mrs. Cain, and had been the one to find out about her rather seamy past—two Vice convictions under a different name, and one hospitalization after a rather messy backstreet abortion. Turned out Cain knew about his future wife's past, but the Bureau hadn't liked it.

And two nights ago, Bryce had to be the one to tell Cain that he couldn't marry his now-reformed, somewhat religious, beloved. The soon-to-be Mrs. Cain had taken the news hard. She had gone to Bellevue this afternoon after slashing her wrists.

And Bryce had been the one to tell Cain what his former fiancée had done. Just a few hours ago.

Sometimes Bryce hated this job.

Despite his orders, he went into the bathroom, soaked one of Mary's precious company towels in water, and dropped the thing on the spilled milk. Then he pulled on his clothes, and finger-combed his hair.

He was a mess—certainly not the perfect representative of the Bureau. His white shirt was stained with marinara from that night's take-out, and his tie wouldn't keep a crisp knot. The crease had long since left his trousers and his shoes hadn't been shined in weeks. Still, he grabbed his black overcoat, hoping it would hide everything.

He let himself out of the apartment before he remembered the required and much hated hat, went back inside, grabbed the hat as well as his gun and his identification. Jesus, he was tired. He hadn't slept since Mary walked out. Mary, who had been vetted by the FBI and who had passed with flying colors. Mary, who had turned out to be more of a liability than any former hooker ever could have been.

And now, because of her, he was heading toward something big, and he was one-tenth as sharp as usual.

All he could hope for was that the SAC had overreacted. And he had a hunch—a two in the morning, get-your-ass-over-there-now hunch—that the SAC hadn't overreacted at all.

———

Attorney General Robert F. Kennedy sat in his favorite chair near the fire in his library. The house was quiet even though his wife and eight children were asleep upstairs. Outside, the rolling landscape was covered in a light dusting of snow—rare for McLean, Virginia even at this time of year.

He held a book in his left hand, his finger marking the spot. The Greeks had comforted him in the few months since Jack died, but lately Kennedy had discovered Camus.

He had been about to copy a passage into his notebook when the phone rang. At first he sighed, feeling all of the exhaustion that had weighed on him since the assassination. He didn't want to answer the phone. He didn't want to be bothered—not now, not ever again.

But this was the direct line from the White House and if he didn't answer it, someone else in the house would.

He set the Camus book face down on his chair and crossed to the desk before the third ring. He answered with a curt, "Yes?"

"Attorney General Kennedy, sir?" The voice on the

other end sounded urgent. The voice sounded familiar to him even though he couldn't place it.

"Yes?"

"This is Special Agent John Haskell. You asked me to contact you, sir, if I heard anything important about Director Hoover, no matter what the time."

Kennedy leaned against the desk. He had made that request back when his brother had been president, back when Kennedy had been the first attorney general since the 1920s who actually demanded accountability from Hoover.

Since Lyndon Johnson had taken over the presidency, accountability had gone by the wayside. These days Hoover rarely returned Kennedy's phone calls.

"Yes, I did tell you that," Kennedy said, resisting the urge to add, but *I don't care about that old man any longer.*

"Sir, there are rumors—credible ones—that Director Hoover has died in New York."

Kennedy froze. For a moment, he flashed back to that unseasonably warm afternoon when he'd sat just outside with the federal attorney for New York City, Robert Morganthau and the chief of Morganthau's criminal division, Silvio Mollo, talking about prosecuting various organized crime figures.

Kennedy could still remember the glint of the sunlight on the swimming pool, the taste of the tuna fish sandwich Ethel had brought him, the way the men—despite their topic—had seemed lighthearted.

Then the phone rang, and J. Edgar Hoover was on the line. Kennedy almost didn't take the call, but he did and Hoover's cold voice said, *I have news for you. The President's been shot.*

Kennedy had always disliked Hoover, but since that day, that awful day in the bright sunshine, he hated that fat bastard. Not once—not in that call, not in the subsequent calls—did Hoover express condolences or show a shred of human concern.

"Credible rumors?" Kennedy repeated, knowing he probably sounded as cold as Hoover had three months ago, and not caring. He'd chosen Haskell as his liaison precisely because the man didn't like Hoover either. Kennedy had needed someone inside Hoover's hierarchy, unbeknownst to Hoover, which was difficult since Hoover kept his hand in everything. Haskell was one of the few who fit the bill.

"Yes, sir, quite credible."

"Then why haven't I received official contact?"

"I'm not even sure the President knows, sir."

Kennedy leaned against the desk. "Why not, if the rumors are credible?"

"Um, because, sir, um, it seems Associate Director Tolson was also shot, and um, they were, um, in a rather suspect area."

Kennedy closed his eyes. All of Washington knew that Tolson was the closest thing Hoover had to a wife. The two old men had been life-long companions. Even though they didn't live together, they had every meal together. Tolson had been Hoover's hatchet man until the last year or so, when Tolson's health hadn't permitted it.

Then a word Haskell used sank in. "You said shot."

"Yes, sir."

"Is Tolson dead too then?"

"And three other people in the neighborhood," Haskell said.

"My God." Kennedy ran a hand over his face. "But they think this is personal?"

"Yes, sir."

"Because of the location of the shooting?"

"Yes, sir. It seems there was an exclusive gathering in a nearby building. You know the type, sir."

Kennedy didn't know the type—at least not through personal experience. But he'd heard of places like that, where the rich, famous and deviant could spend time with each other, and do whatever it was they liked to do in something approaching privacy.

"So," he said, "the bureau's trying to figure out how to cover this up."

"Or at least contain it, sir."

Without Hoover or Tolson. No one in the bureau was going to know what to do.

Kennedy's hand started to shake. "What about the files?"

"Files, sir?"

"Hoover's confidential files. Has anyone secured them?"

"Not yet, sir. But I'm sure someone has called Miss Gandy."

Helen Gandy was Hoover's long-time secretary. She had been his right hand as long as Tolson had operated that hatchet.

"So procedure's being followed," Kennedy said, then frowned. If procedure were being followed, shouldn't the acting head of the bureau be calling him?

"No, sir. But the Director put some private instructions in place should he be killed or incapacitated. Private emergency instructions. And those involve letting Miss Gandy know before anyone else."

Even me, Kennedy thought. *Hoover's nominal boss.* "She's not there yet, right?"

"No, sir."

"Do you know where those files are?" Kennedy asked, trying not to let desperation into his voice.

"I've made it my business to know, sir." There was a pause and then Haskell lowered his voice. "They're in Miss Gandy's office, sir."

Not Hoover's like everyone thought. For the first time in months, Kennedy felt a glimmer of hope. "Secure those files."

"Sir?"

"Do whatever it takes. I want them out of there, and I

want someone to secure Hoover's house too. I'm acting on the orders of the President. If anyone tells you that they are doing the same, they're mistaken. The President made his wishes clear on this point. He often said if anything happens to that old queer—" And here Kennedy deliberately used LBJ's favorite phrase for Hoover "—then we need those files before they can get into the wrong hands."

"I'm on it, sir."

"I can't stress to you the importance of this," Kennedy said. In fact, he couldn't talk about the importance at all. Those files could ruin his brother's legacy. The secrets in there could bring down Kennedy too, and his entire family.

"And if the rumors about the Director's death are wrong, sir?"

Kennedy felt a shiver of fear. "Are they?"

"I seriously doubt it."

"Then let me worry about that."

And about what LBJ would do when he found out. Because the president upon whose orders Kennedy acted wasn't the current one. Kennedy was following the orders of the only man he believed should be president at the moment.

His brother, Jack.

———

The scene wasn't hard to find; a coroner's van blocked the entrance to the alley. Bryce walked quickly, already cold, his heartburn worse than it had been when he had gone to bed.

The neighborhood was in transition. An urban renewal project had knocked down some wonderful turn of the century buildings that had become eyesores. But so far, the buildings that had replaced them were the worst kind of modern—all planes and angles and white with few windows.

In the buildings closest to the park, the lights worked and the streets looked safe. But here, on a side street not far from the construction, the city's shady side showed. The dirty snow was piled against the curb, the streets were dark, and nothing seemed inhabited except that alley with the coroner's van blocking the entrance.

The coroner's van and at least one unmarked car. No press, which surprised him. He shoved his gloved hands in the pockets of his overcoat even though it was against FBI dress code, and slipped between the van and the wall of a grimy brick building.

The alley smelled of old urine and fresh blood. Two beat cops blocked his way until he showed identification. Then, like people usually did, they parted as if he could burn them.

The bodies had fallen side by side in the center of the

alley. They looked posed, with their arms up, their legs in classic P position—one leg bent, the other straight. They looked like they could fit perfectly on the dead body diagrams the FBI used to put out in the 1930s. He wondered if they had fallen like this or if this had been the result of the coroner's tampering.

The coroner had messed with other parts of the crime scene—if, indeed, he had been the one who put the garbage can lids on the ice and set battery-powered lamps on them. The warmth of the lamps was melting the ice and sending runnels of water into a nearby grate.

"I hope to hell someone thought to photograph the scene before you melted it," he said.

The coroner and the two cops who had been crouching beside the bodies stood up guiltily. The coroner looked at the garbage can lids and closed his eyes. Then he took a deep breath, opened them, and snapped his fingers at the assistant who was waiting beside a gurney.

"Camera," he said.

"That's Crime Scene's—." the assistant began, then saw everyone looking at him. He glanced at the van. "Never mind."

He walked behind the bodies, further disturbing the scene. Bryce's mouth thinned in irritation. The cops who stood were in plain clothes.

"Detectives," Bryce said, holding his identification,

"Special Agent Frank Bryce of the FBI. I've been told to secure this scene. More of my people will be here shortly."

He hoped that last was true. He had no idea who was coming or when they would arrive.

"Good," said the younger detective, a tall man with broad shoulders and an all-American jaw. "The sooner we get out of here the better."

Bryce had never gotten that reaction from a detective before. Usually the detectives were territorial, always reminding him that this was New York City and that the scene belonged to them.

The other detective, older, face grizzled by time and work, held out his gloved hand. "Forgive my partner's rudeness. I'm Seamus O'Reilly. He's Joseph McAllister and we'll help you in any way we can."

"I appreciate it," Bryce said, taking O'Reilly's hand and shaking it. "I guess the first thing you can do is tell me what we've got."

"A hell of a mess, that's for sure," said McAllister. "You'll understand when...."

His voice trailed off as his partner took out two long, old-fashioned wallets and handed them to Bryce.

Bryce took them, feeling confused. Then he opened the first, saw the familiar badge, and felt his breath catch. Two FBI agents, in this alley? Shot side-by-side? He looked up, saw the darkened windows.

There used to be rumors about this neighborhood. Some exclusive private sex parties used to be held here, and his old partner had always wanted to visit one just to see if it was a hotbed of Communists like some of the agents had claimed. Bryce had begged off. He was an investigator, not a voyeur.

The two detectives were staring at him, as if they expected more from him. He still had the wallet open in his hand. If the dead men were New York agents, he would know them. He hated solving the deaths of people he knew.

But he steeled himself, looked at the identification, and felt the blood leave his face. His skin grew cold and for a moment he felt lightheaded.

"No," he said.

The detectives still stared at him.

He swallowed. "Have you done a visual i.d.?"

Hoover was recognizable. His picture was on everything. Sometimes Bryce thought Hoover was more famous than the president—any president. He'd certainly been in power longer.

"Faces are gone," O'Reilly said.

"Exit wounds," the coroner added from beside the bodies. His assistant had returned and was taking pictures, the flash showing just how much melt had happened since the coroner arrived.

"Shot in the back of the head?" Bryce blinked. He was

tired and his brain was working slowly, but something about the shots didn't match with the body positions.

"If they came out that door," O'Reilly said as he indicated a dark metal door almost hidden in the side of the brick building, "then the shooters had to be waiting beside it."

"Your crime scene people haven't arrived yet, I take it?" Bryce asked.

"No," the coroner said. "They think it's a fag kill. They'll get here when they get here."

Bryce clenched his left fist and had to remind himself to let the fingers loose.

O'Reilly saw the reaction. "Sorry about that," he said, shooting a glare at the coroner. "I'm sure the director was here on business."

Funny business. But Bryce didn't say that. The rumors about Hoover had been around since Bryce joined the FBI just after the war. Hoover quashed them, like he quashed any criticism, but it seemed like the criticism got made, no matter what.

Bryce opened the other wallet, but he already had a guess as to who was beside Hoover, and his guess turned out to be right.

"You want to tell me why your crime scene people believe this is a homosexual killing?" Bryce asked, trying not to let what Mary called his FBI tone into his voice. If Hoover was still alive and this was some kind of plant,

Hoover would want to crush the source of this assumption. Bryce would make sure that the source was worth pursuing before going any farther.

"Neighborhood, mostly," McAllister said. "There're a couple of bars, mostly high-end. You have to know someone to get in. Then there's the party, held every week upstairs. Some of the most important men in the city show up at it, or so they used to say in Vice when they told us to stay away."

Bryce nodded, letting it go at that.

"We need your crime scene people here ASAP, and a lot more cops so that we can protect what's left of this scene, in case these men turn out to be who their identification says they are. You search the bodies to see if this was the only identification on them?"

O'Reilly started. He clearly hadn't thought of that. Probably had been too shocked by the first wallets that he found.

The younger detective had already gone back to the bodies. The coroner put out a hand, and did the searching himself.

"You think this was a plant?" O'Reilly asked.

"I don't know what to think," Bryce said. "I'm not here to think. I'm here to make sure everything goes smoothly."

And to make sure the case goes to the FBI. Those words hung unspoken between the two of them. Not that O'Reilly objected, and now Bryce could understand why. This case would be a political nightmare, and no good detective wanted to be in the middle of it.

"How come there's no press?" Bryce asked O'Reilly. "You manage to get rid of them somehow?"

"Fag kill," the coroner said.

Bryce was getting tired of those words. His fist had clenched again, and he had to work at unclenching it.

"Ignore him," O'Reilly said softly. "He's an asshole and the best coroner in the city."

"I heard that," the coroner said affably. "There's no other identification on either of them."

O'Reilly's shoulders slumped, as if he'd been hoping for a different outcome. Bryce should have been hoping as well, but he hadn't been. He had known that Hoover was in town. The entire New York bureau knew, since Hoover always took it over when he arrived—breezing in, giving instructions, making sure everything was just the way he wanted it.

"Before this gets too complicated," O'Reilly said, "you want to see the other bodies?"

"Other bodies?" Bryce felt numb. He could use some caffeine now, but Hoover had ordered agents not to drink coffee on the job. Getting coffee now felt almost disrespectful.

"We got three more." O'Reilly took a deep breath. "And just before you arrived, I got word that they're agents too."

Special Agent John Haskell had just installed six of his best agents outside the Director's suite of offices when a small woman showed up, key clutched in her gloved right hand. Helen Gandy, the Director's secretary, looked up at Haskell with the coldest stare he'd ever seen outside of the Director's.

"May I go into my office, Agent Haskell?" Her voice was just as cold. She didn't look upset, and if he hadn't known that she never stayed past five unless directed by Hoover himself, Haskell would have thought she was coming back from a prolonged work break.

"I'm sorry, Ma'am," he said. "No one is allowed inside. President's orders."

"Really?" God, that voice was chilling. He remembered the first time he'd heard it, when he'd been brought to this suite of offices as a brand-new agent, after getting his "Meet the Boss" training before his introduction to the Director. She'd frightened him more than Hoover had.

"Yes, Ma'am. The President says no one can enter."

"Surely he didn't mean me."

Surely he did. But Haskell bit the comment back. "I'm sorry, Ma'am."

"I have a few personal items that I'd like to get, if you don't mind. And the Director instructed me that in the case of..." and for the first time she paused. Her voice didn't break nor did she clear her throat. But she seemed to need a moment to gather herself. "In case of emergency, I was to remove some of his personal items as well."

"If you could tell me what they are, Ma'am, I'll get them."

Her eyes narrowed. "The Director doesn't like others to touch his possessions."

"I'm sorry, Ma'am," he said gently. "But I don't think that matters any longer."

Any other woman would have broken down. After all, she had worked for the old man for forty-five years, side-by-side, every day. Never marrying, not because they had a relationship—Helen Gandy, more than anyone, probably knew the truth behind the Director's relationship with the Associate Director—but because for Helen Gandy, just like for the Director himself, the FBI was her entire life.

"It matters," she said. "Now if you'll excuse me..."

She tried to wriggle past him. She was wiry and stronger than he expected. He had to put out an arm to block her.

"Ma'am," he said in the gentlest tone he could summon, "the President's orders supersede the Director's."

How often had he wanted to say that over the years? How often had he wanted to remind everyone in the Bureau that the President led the Free World, not J. Edgar Hoover.

"In this instance," she snapped, "they do not."

"Ma'am, I'd hate to have some agents restrain you." Although he wasn't sure about that. She had never been nice to him or to anyone he knew. She'd always been sharp or rude. "You're distraught."

"I am not." She clipped each word.

"You are because I say you are, Ma'am."

She raised her chin. For a moment, he thought she hadn't understood. But she finally did.

The balance of power had shifted. At the moment, it was on his side.

"Do I have to call the president then to get my personal effects?" she asked.

But they both knew she wasn't talking about her personal things. And the President was smart enough to know that as well. As hungry to get those files as the Attorney General had seemed despite his Eastern reserve, the President would be utterly ravenous. He wouldn't let some old skirt, as he'd been known to call Miss Gandy, get in his way.

"Go ahead," Haskell said. "Feel free to use the phone in the office across the hall."

She glared at him, then turned on one foot and marched down the corridor. But she didn't head toward a phone—at least not one he could see.

He wondered who she would call. The President wouldn't listen. The Attorney General had issued the order in the president's name. Maybe she would contact one of

Hoover's Assistant Directors, the four or five men that Hoover had in his pocket.

Haskell had been waiting for them. But word still hadn't spread through the Bureau. The only reason he knew was because he'd received a call from the SAC of the New York office. New York hated the Director, mostly because the old man went there so often and harassed them.

Someone had probably figured out that there was a crisis from the moment that Haskell had brought his people in to secure the Director's suite. But no one would know that the Director was dead until Miss Gandy made the calls or until someone in the Bureau started along the chain of command—the one designated in the book Hoover had written all those years ago.

Haskell crossed his arms. Sometimes he wished he hadn't let the A.G. know how he felt about the Director. Sometimes he wished he were still a humble assistant, the man who had joined the FBI because he wanted to be a top cop like his hero J. Edgar Hoover.

A man who, it turned out, never made a real arrest or fired a gun or even understood investigation.

There was a lot to admire about the Director—no matter what you said, he'd built a hell of an agency almost from scratch—but he wasn't the man his press made him out to be.

And that was the source of Haskell's disillusionment.

He'd wanted to be a top cop. Instead, he snooped into homes and businesses and sometimes even investigated fairly blameless people, looking for a mistake in their past.

Since he'd been transferred to FBIHQ, he hadn't done any real investigating at all. His arrests had slowed, his cases dwindled.

And he'd found himself investigating his boss, trying to find out where the legend ended and the man began. Once he realized that the old man was just a bureaucrat who had learned where all the bodies were buried and used that to make everyone bow to his bidding, Haskell was ripe for the undercover work the A.G. had asked him to do.

Only now he wasn't undercover any more. Now he was standing in the open before the Director's cache of secrets, on the President's orders, hoping that no one would call his bluff.

———

As O'Reilly led him to the limousine, Bryce surreptitiously checked his watch. He'd already been on scene for half an hour, and no back-up had arrived. If he was supposed to secure everything and chase off the NYPD, he'd need some manpower.

But for now, he wanted to see the extent of the problem. The night had gotten colder, and this street was even darker than the street he'd walked down. All of the streetlights were out. The only light came from some porch bulbs above a few entrances. He could barely make out the limousine at the end of the block, and then only because he could see the shadowy forms of the two beat cops standing at the scene, their squad cars parking the limo in.

As he got closer, he recognized the shape of the limo. It was thicker than most limos and rode lower to the ground because it was encased in an extra frame, making it bullet-proof. Supposedly, the glass would all be bulletproof as well.

"You said the driver was shot inside the limo?" Bryce asked.

"That's what they told me," O'Reilly said. "I wasn't called to this scene. We were brought in because of the two men in the alley. Even then we were called late."

Bryce nodded. He remembered the coroner's bigotry. "Is that standard procedure for cases involving minorities?"

O'Reilly gave him a sideways glance. Bryce couldn't read O'Reilly's expression in the dark.

"We're overtaxed," O'Reilly said after a moment. "Some cases don't get the kind of treatment they deserve."

"Limo drivers," Bryce said.

"If he'd been killed in the parking garage under the Plaza maybe," O'Reilly said. "But not because of who he was. But because of where he was."

Bryce nodded. He knew how the world worked. He

didn't like it. He spoke up against it too many times, which was why he was on shaky ground at the Bureau.

Then his already upset stomach clenched. Maybe he wasn't going to get back-up. Maybe they'd put him on his own here to claim he'd botched the investigation, so that they would be able to cover it up.

He couldn't concentrate on that now. What he had to do was take good notes, make the best case he could, and keep a copy of every damn thing—maybe in more than one place.

"You were called in because of the possibility that the men in the alley could be important," Bryce said.

"That's my guess," O'Reilly said.

"What about the others down the block? Has anyone taken those cases?"

"Probably not," O'Reilly said. "Those bars, you know. It's department policy. The coroner checks bodies in the suspect area, and decides, based on...um...evidence of...um...

activity...whether or not to bring in detectives."

Bryce frowned. He almost asked what the coroner was checking for when he figured out that it was evidence on the body itself, evidence not of the crime, but of certain kinds of sex acts. If that evidence was present, apparently no one thought it worthwhile to investigate the crime.

"You'd think the city would revise that," Bryce said. "A

lot of people live dual lives—productive and interesting people."

"Yeah," O'Reilly said. "You'd think. Especially after tonight."

Bryce grinned. He was liking this grizzled cop more and more.

O'Reilly spoke to the beat cops, then motioned Bryce to the limo. As Bryce approached, O'Reilly trained his flashlight on the driver's side.

The window wasn't broken like Bryce had expected. It had been rolled down.

"You got here one James Crawford," said one of the beat cops. "He got identification says he's a feebee, but I ain't never heard of no colored feebee."

"There's only four," Bryce said dryly. And they all worked for Hoover as his personal housekeepers or drivers. "Can I see that identification?"

The beat cop handed him a wallet that matched the ones on Tolson and Hoover. Inside was a badge and identification for James Crawford as well as family photographs. Neither Tolson nor Hoover had had any photographs in their wallets.

Bryce motioned O'Reilly to move a little closer to the body. The head was tilted toward the window. The right side of the skull was gone, the hair glistening with drying blood. With one gloved finger, Bryce pushed the head upright. A single entrance wound above the left ear had caused the damage.

"Brunner says the shots are the same caliber," O'Reilly said.

It took Bryce a moment to realize that Brunner was the coroner.

Bryce carefully searched Crawford but didn't find the man's weapon. Nor could he find a holster or any way to carry a weapon.

"It looks like he wasn't carrying a weapon," Bryce said.

"Neither were the two in the alley," O'Reilly said, and Bryce appreciated his caution in not identifying the other two corpses. "You'd think they would have been."

Bryce shook his head. "They were known for not carrying weapons. But you'd think their driver would have one."

"Maybe they had protection," O'Reilly said.

And Bryce's mouth went dry. Of course they did. The office always joked about who would get HooverWatch on each trip. He'd had to do it a few times.

Agents on HooverWatch followed strict rules, like everything else with Hoover. Remain close enough to see the men entering and exiting an area, stop any suspicious characters, and yet somehow remain inconspicuous.

"You said there were two others shot?"

"Yeah. A block or so from here." O'Reilly waved a hand vaguely down the street.

"Pulled out of one car or two?"

"Not my case," O'Reilly said.

"Two," said the beat cop. "Black sedans. Could barely see them on this cruddy street."

HooverWatch. Bryce swallowed hard, that bile back. Of course. He probably knew the men who were shot.

"Let's look," he said. "You two, make sure the coroner's man photographs this scene before he leaves."

"Yessir," said the second beat cop. He hadn't spoken before.

"And don't let anyone near this scene unless I give the o.k.," Bryce said.

"How come this guy's in charge?" the talkative beat cop asked O'Reilly.

O'Reilly grinned. "Because he's a feebee."

"I'm sorry," the beat cop said automatically turning to Bryce. "I didn't know, sir."

Feebee was an insult—or at least some in the Bureau thought so. Bryce didn't mind it. Any more than he minded when some rookie said "Sack" when he meant "Ess-Ay-Cee." Shorthand worked, sometimes better than people wanted it to.

"Point me in the right direction," he said to the talkative cop.

The cop nodded south. "One block down, sir. You can't miss it. We got guys on those scenes too, but we weren't so sure it was important. You know. We coulda missed stuff."

In other words, they hadn't buttoned up the scene immediately. They'd waited for the coroner to make his verdict, and he probably hadn't, not with the three new corpses nearby.

Bryce took one last look at James Crawford. The man had rolled down his window, despite the cold, and in a bad section of town.

He leaned forward. Underneath the faint scent of cordite and mingled with the thicker smell of blood was the smell of a cigar.

He took the flashlight from O'Reilly and trained it on the dirty snow against the curb. It had been trampled by everyone coming to this crime scene.

He crouched, and poked just a little, finding three fairly fresh cigarette butts.

As he stood, he said to the beat cops, "When the scene of the crime guys get here, make sure they take everything from the curb."

O'Reilly was watching him. The beat cops were frowning, but they nodded.

Bryce handed O'Reilly back his flashlight and headed down the street.

"You think he was smoking and tossing the butts out the window?" O'Reilly asked.

"Either that," Bryce said, "or he rolled his window down to talk to someone. And if someone was pointing a gun at him, he wouldn't have done it. This vehicle was armored. He had a better chance starting it up and driving away than he did cooperating."

"If he wasn't smoking," O'Reilly said, "he knew his killer."

"Yeah," Bryce said. And he was pretty sure that was going to make his job a whole hell of a lot harder.

————

Kennedy took the elevator up to the fifth floor of the Justice Department. He probably should have stayed home, but he simply couldn't. He needed to get into those files and he needed to do so before anyone else.

As he strode into the corridor he shared with the Director of the FBI, he saw Helen Gandy hurry in the other direction. She looked like she had just come from the beauty salon. He had never seen her look anything less than completely put together but he was surprised by her perfect appearance on this night, after the news that her long-time boss was dead.

Kennedy tugged at the overcoat he'd put on over his favorite sweater. He hadn't taken the time to change or even comb his hair. He probably looked as tousled as he had in the days after Jack died.

Although, for the first time in three months, he felt like he had a purpose. He didn't know how long this feeling would last, or how long he wanted it to. But this death had given him an odd kind of hope that control was coming back into his world.

Haskell stood in front of the Director's office suite, arms crossed. The Director's suite was just down the corridor from the Attorney General's offices. It felt odd to go toward Hoover's domain instead of his own.

Haskell looked relieved when he saw Kennedy.

"Was that the dragon lady I just saw?" Kennedy asked.

"She wanted to get some personal effects from her office," Haskell said.

"Did you let her?"

"You said the orders were to secure it, so I have."

"Excellent." Kennedy glanced in both directions and saw no one. "Make sure your staff continues to protect the doors. I'm going inside."

"Sir?" Haskell raised his eyebrows.

"This may not be the right place," Kennedy said. "I'm worried that he moved everything to his house."

The lie came easily. Kennedy would have heard if Hoover had moved files to his own home. But Haskell didn't know that.

Haskell moved away from the door. It was unlocked. Two more agents stood inside, guarding the interior doors.

"Give me a minute, please, gentlemen," Kennedy said.

The men nodded and went outside.

Kennedy stopped and took a deep breath. He had been

in Miss Gandy's office countless times, but he had never really looked at it. He'd always been staring at the door to Hoover's inner sanctum, waiting for it to open and the old man to come out.

That office was interesting. In the antechamber, Hoover had memorabilia and photographs from his major cases. He even had the Plaster of Paris death mask of John Dillinger on display. It was a ghastly thing, which made Kennedy think of the way that English kings used to keep severed heads on the entrance to London Bridge to warn traitors of their potential fate.

But this office had always looked like a waiting room to him. Nothing very special. The woman behind the desk was the focal point. Jack had been the one who nicknamed her the dragon lady and had even called her that to her face once, only with his trademark grin, so infectious that she hadn't made a sound or a grimace in protest.

Of course, she hadn't smiled back either.

Her desk was clear except for a blotter, a telephone, and a jar of pens. A typewriter sat on a credenza with paper stacked beside it.

But it wasn't the desk that interested him the most. It was the floor-to-ceiling filing cabinets and storage bins. He walked to them. Instead of the typical system—marked by letters of the alphabet—this one had numbers that were clearly part of a code.

He pulled open the nearest drawer, and found row after

row of accordion files, each with its own number, and manila folders with the first number set followed by another. He cursed softly under his breath.

Of course the old dog wouldn't file his confidentials by name. He'd use a secret code. The old man liked nothing more than his secrets.

Still, Kennedy opened half a dozen drawers just to see if the system continued throughout. And it wasn't until he got to a bin near the corner of the desk that he found a file labeled "Obscene."

His hand shook as he pulled it out. Jack, for all his brilliance, had been sexually insatiable. Back when their brother Joe was still alive and no one ever thought Jack would be running for president, Jack had had an affair with a Danish émigré named Inga Arvad. Inga Binga, as Jack used to call her, was married to a man with ties to Hitler. She'd even met and liked Der Fuhrer, and had said so in print.

She'd been the target of FBI surveillance as a possible spy, and during that surveillance who should turn up in her bed but a young naval lieutenant whose father had once been Ambassador to England. The Ambassador, as he preferred to be called even by his sons, found out about the affair, told Jack in no uncertain terms to end it, and then to make sure he did by getting him assigned to a PT boat in the Pacific, as far from Inga Binga as possible.

Kennedy had always suspected that Hoover had leaked

the information to the Ambassador, but he hadn't known for certain until Jack became President when Hoover told them. Hoover had been surveilling all of the Kennedy children at the Ambassador's request. He'd given Kennedy a list of scandalous items as a sample, and hoped that would control the president and his brother.

It might have controlled Jack, but Hoover hadn't known Kennedy very well. Kennedy had told Hoover that if any of this information made it into the press, then other things would appear in print as well, things like the strange FBI budget items for payments covering Hoover's visits to the track or the fact that Hoover made some interesting friends, mobster friends, when he was vacationing in Palm Beach.

It wasn't quite a Mexican stand-off—Jack was really afraid of the old man—but it gave Kennedy more power than any Attorney General had had over Hoover since the beginnings of the Roosevelt administration.

But now Kennedy needed those files, and he had a hunch Hoover would label them obscene.

Kennedy opened the file, and was shocked to see Richard Nixon's name on the sheets inside. Kennedy thumbed through quickly, not caring what dirt they'd found on that loser. Nixon couldn't win an election after his defeat in 1960. He'd even told the press after he lost a California race that they wouldn't have him to kick around any more.

Yet Hoover had kept the files, just to be safe.

That old bastard really and truly had known where all the bodies were buried. And it wouldn't be easy to find them.

Kennedy took a deep breath. He stood, shoved his hands in his pockets, and surveyed the walls of files. It would take days to search each folder. He didn't have days. He probably didn't have hours.

But he was Hoover's immediate supervisor, whether the old man had recognized it or not. Hoover answered to him. Which meant that the files belonged to the Justice Department, of which the FBI was only one small part.

He glanced at his watch. No one pounded on the door. He probably had until dawn before someone tried to stop him. If he was really lucky, no one would think of the files until mid-morning.

He went to the door and beckoned Haskell inside.

"We're taking the files to my office," he said.

"All of them, sir?"

"All of them. These first, then whatever is in Hoover's office, and then any other confidential files you can find."

Haskell looked up the wall as if he couldn't believe the command. "That'll take some time, sir."

"Not if you get a lot of people to help."

"Sir, I thought you wanted to keep this secret."

He did. But it wouldn't remain secret for long. So he

had to control when the information got out—just like he had to control the information itself.

"Get this done as quickly as possible," he said.

Haskell nodded and turned the doorknob, but Kennedy stopped him before he went out.

"These are filed by code," he said. "Do you know where the key is?"

"I was told that Miss Gandy had the keys to everything from codes to offices," Haskell said.

Kennedy felt a shiver run through him. Knowing Hoover, he would have made sure he had the key to the Attorney General's office as well.

"Do you have any idea where she might have kept the code keys?" Kennedy asked.

"No," Haskell said. "I wasn't part of the need-to-know group. I already knew too much."

Kennedy nodded. He appreciated how much Haskell knew. It had gotten him this far.

"On your way out," Kennedy said, "call building maintenance and have them change all the locks in my office."

"Yes, sir." Haskell kept his hand on the doorknob. "Are you sure you want to do this, sir? Couldn't you just change the locks here? Wouldn't that secure everything for the President?"

"Everyone in Washington wants these files," Kennedy said. "They're going to come to this office suite. They won't think of mine."

"Until they heard that you moved everything."

Kennedy nodded. "And then they'll know how futile their quest really is."

———

The final crime scene was a mess. The bodies were already gone—probably inside the coroner's van that blocked the alley a few blocks back. It had taken Bryce nearly a half an hour to find someone who knew what the scene had looked like when the police had first arrived.

That someone was Officer Ralph Voight. He was tall and trim, with a pristine uniform despite the fact that he'd been on duty all night.

O'Reilly was the one who convinced him to talk with Bryce. Voight was the first to show the traditional animosity between the NYPD and the FBI, but that was because Voight didn't know who had died only a few blocks away.

Bryce had Voight walk him through the crime scene. The buildings on this street were boarded up, and the lights burned out. Broken glass littered the sidewalk—and it hadn't come from this particular crime. Rusted beer cans, half buried in the ice piles, cluttered each stoop like passed-out drunks.

"Okay," Voight said, using his flashlight as a pointer, "we come up on these two cars first."

The two sedans were parked against the curb, one behind the other. The sedans were too nice for the neighborhood—new, black, without a dent. Bryce recognized them as FBI issue—he had access to a sedan like that himself when he needed it.

He patted his pocket, was disgusted to realize he'd left his notebook at the apartment, and turned to O'Reilly. "You got paper? I need those plates."

O'Reilly nodded. He pulled out a notebook and wrote down the plate numbers.

"They just looked wrong," Voight was saying. "So we stopped, figuring maybe someone needed assistance."

He pointed the flashlight across the street. The squad had stopped directly across from the two cars.

"That's when we seen the first body."

He walked them to the middle of the street. This part of the city hadn't been plowed regularly and a layer of ice had built over the pavement. A large pool of blood had melted through that ice, leaving its edges reddish black and revealing the pavement below.

"The guy was face down, hands out like he'd tried to catch himself."

"Face gone?" Bryce asked, thinking maybe it was a head shot like the others.

"No. Turns out he was shot in the back."

Bryce glanced at O'Reilly, whose lips had thinned. This one was different. Because it was the first? Or because it was unrelated?

"We pull our weapons, scan to see if we see anyone else, which we don't. The door's open on the first sedan, but we didn't see anyone in the dome light. And we didn't see anyone obvious on the street, but it's really dark here and the flashlights don't reach far." Voight turned his light toward the block with the parked limousine, but neither the car nor the sidewalk was visible from this distance.

"So we go to the cars, careful now, and find the other body right there."

He flashed his light on the curb beside the door to the first sedan.

"This one's on his back and the door is open. We figure he was getting out when he got plugged. Then the other guy—maybe he was outside his car trying to help this guy with I don't know what, some car trouble or something, then his buddy gets hit, so he runs for cover across the street and gets nailed. End of story."

"Did you check to see if the cars start?" O'Reilly asked. Bryce nodded that was going to be his next question as well.

"I'm not supposed to touch the scene, sir," Voight said with some resentment. "We secured the area, figured everything was okay, then called it in."

"Did you hear the other shots?"

"No," Voight said. "I know we got three more up there, and you'd think I'd've heard the shooting if something happened, but I didn't. And as you can tell, it's damn quiet around here at night."

Bryce could tell. He didn't like the silence in the middle of the city. Neighborhoods that got quiet like this so close to dawn were usually among the worst. The early morning maintenance workers, and the delivery drivers stayed away whenever they could.

He peered in the sedan, then pulled the door open. The interior light went on, and there was blood all over the front seat and steering wheel. There were styrofoam coffee cups on both sides of the little rise between the seats. And the keys were in the ignition. Like all Bureau issue, the car was an automatic.

Carefully, so that he wouldn't disturb anything important in the scene, he turned the key. The sedan purred to life, sounding well-tuned just like it was supposed to.

"Check to see if there are other problems," Bryce said to O'Reilly. "A flat maybe."

Although Bryce knew there wouldn't be one. He shut off the ignition.

"You didn't see the interior light when you pulled up?" he asked Voight.

"Yeah, but it was dim," Voight said. "That's why I figured there was car problems. I figured they left the lights on so they could see."

Bryce nodded. He understood the assumption. He backed out of the sedan, then walked around it, shining his own flashlight at the hole in the ice, and then back at the first sedan.

Directly across.

He walked to the second sedan. Its interior was clean—no styrofoam cups, no wadded up food containers, no notebooks. Not even some tools hastily pulled to help the other drivers in need.

He let out a small sigh. He finally figured out what was bothering him.

"You find weapons on the two men?" he asked Voight.

"Yes, sir."

"Holstered?"

"The guy by the car. The other one had his in his right hand. We figured we just happened on the scene or someone would have taken the weapon."

Or not. People tended to hide for a while after shots were fired, particularly if they had nothing to do with the shootings but might get blamed anyway.

Bryce tried to open the passenger door on the second sedan, but it was locked. He walked around to the driver's door. Locked as well.

"No one looked inside this car?"

"No, sir. We figured crime scene would do it."

"But they haven't been here yet?" Bryce asked.

"It's the neighborhood, sir. Right there—" Voight

aimed his flashlight at stairs heading down to a lower level "—is one of those men-only clubs, you know? The kind that you go to when you're...you know...looking for other men."

Bryce felt a flash of irritation. He'd been running into this all night. "Okay. What I'm hearing in a sideways way from every representative of the NYPD on this scene is that crimes in this neighborhood don't get investigated."

Voight sputtered. "They get investigated—"

"They get investigated," O'Reilly said, "enough to tell the families they probably want to back off. You heard Brunner. That's what most in the department call it. The rest of us, we call them lifestyle kills. And we get in trouble if we waste too many resources on them."

"Lovely," Bryce said dryly. His philosophy, which had gotten him in trouble with the Bureau more than once, was that all crimes deserved investigation, no matter how distasteful you found the victims. Which was why he kept getting moved, from communists to reviewing wire-taps to digging dirt on other agents.

And that was probably why he was here. He was expendable.

"Did you find car keys on either of the victims?" Bryce asked.

"No, sir," Voight said. "And I helped the coroner when he first arrived."

"Then start looking. See if they got dropped in the struggle."

Although Bryce doubted they had.

"I got something to jimmy the lock in my car," O'Reilly said.

Bryce nodded. Then he stood back, surveying the whole thing. He didn't like how he was thinking. It was making his heartburn grow worse.

But it was the only thing that made sense.

Agents worked HooverWatch in pairs. There were two dead agents and two cars. If the second sedan was back-up, there should have been four agents and two cars.

But it didn't look that way. It looked like someone had pulled up behind the HooverWatch vehicle, and got out, carefully locking the door.

Then he went to the door of the HooverWatch car. The driver had got out to talk to him, and the new guy shot him.

At that point, the second HooverWatch agent was an easy target. He scrambled out of the car, grabbed his own weapon, and headed across the street—maybe shooting as he went. The shooter got him, and then casually walked up the street to the limo, which he had to know was there even though he couldn't see it.

As he approached the limo, the limo driver lowered his window. He would have recognized the approaching man, and thought he was going to report on the danger.

Instead, the man shot him, then went to lie in wait for Hoover and Tolson.

Bryce shivered. It would have happened very fast, and long before the beat cops showed up.

The guy in the street had time to bleed out. The limo driver couldn't warn his boss. And the beat cops hadn't heard the shots in the alley, which they would have on such a quiet night.

O'Reilly brought the jimmy, shoved it into the space between the window and the lock, and flipped the lock up with a single movement. Then he opened the door.

No keys in the ignition.

Bryce flipped open the glovebox. Nothing inside but the vehicle registration. Which, as he expected, identified it as an FBI vehicle.

The shooter had planned to come back. He'd planned to drive away in this car. But he got delayed. And by the time he got here, the two beat cops were on scene. He couldn't get his car.

He had to improvise. So he probably walked away or took the subway, hoping the cops would think the extra car belonged to one of the victims.

And that was his mistake.

"How come you guys were here in the middle of the night?" Bryce asked Voight.

Voight swallowed. It was the first sign of nervousness he'd shown. "This is part of our beat."

"But?" Bryce asked.

Voight looked away. "We're supposed to go up Central Park West."

"And you don't."

"Yeah, we do. Just not every time."

"Because?"

"Because I figure, you know, when the bars let out, we could, you know, let our presence be known."

"Prevent a lifestyle kill."

"Yes, sir."

"And you care about this because...?"

"Everyone should," Voight snapped. "Serve and protect, right, sir?"

Voight was touchy. He thought Bryce was accusing him of protecting the lifestyle because he lived it.

"Does your partner like this drive?" Bryce asked.

"He complains, sir, but he lets me do it."

"Have you stopped any crimes?"

"Broken up a few fights," Voight said.

"But not something like this."

"No, sir."

"You don't patrol every night, do you, Voight?"

"No, sir. We get different regions different nights."

"Do you think our killer would have thought that this street was unprotected?"

"It usually is, sir."

O'Reilly was frowning, but not at Voight. At Bryce. "You think this was planned?" O'Reilly asked.

Bryce didn't answer. This was a Bureau matter, and he wasn't sure how the Bureau would handle it.

But he did think the killing was planned. And he had a hunch it would be easy to solve because of the abandoned sedan.

And that abandoned sedan bothered him more than he wanted to admit. Because the presence of that sedan meant only one thing: that the person who had shot all five FBI agents was—almost without a doubt—an FBI agent himself.

Kennedy looked at the bins and the filing cabinets stacked around his office and allowed himself one moment to feel overwhelmed. People ribbed him about the office; he had taken the reception area and made it his, rather than use the standard size office in the back.

As a result, his office was as long as a football field, with stunning windows along the walls. The watercolors painted by his children had been covered by the cabinets. His furniture was pushed aside to make room for the bins, and for the first time, this space felt small.

He put his hands on his hips and wondered how to begin.

Since six agents began moving the filing cabinets across the corridor more than an hour ago, Kennedy had received five phone calls from LBJ's chief of staff. Kennedy hadn't taken one of them. The last had been a direct order to come to the Oval Office.

Kennedy ignored it.

He also ignored the ringing telephone—the White House line—and the messages his own assistant (called in after a short night's sleep) had been bringing to him.

Helen Gandy stood in the corridor, arms crossed, her purse hanging off her wrist, and watching with deep disapproval. Haskell was trying to find out if there were remaining files and where they were. But Kennedy had found the one thing he was looking for: the key.

It was in a large, innocuous index file box inside the lowest drawer of Helen Gandy's desk. Kennedy had brought it into his office and was thumbing through it, hoping to understand it before he got interrupted again.

A man from building maintenance had changed the lock on the door leading into the interior offices, and was working on the main doors now that the files were all inside. Kennedy figured he'd have his own office secure by seven a.m.

Then he heard a rustling in the hallway, a lot of startled, "Mr. President, sir!" followed by official, "Make way for the President," and instinctively he turned toward the door. The maintenance man was leaning out of it, the door knob loose in his hand.

"Where the fuck is that bastard?" Lyndon Baines Johnson's voice echoed from the corridor. "Doesn't anyone in this building have balls enough to tell him that he works for me?"

Even though the question was rhetorical, someone tried to answer. Kennedy heard something about "your orders, sir."

"Horseshit!" Then LBJ stood in the doorway. Two secret service agents flanked him. He motioned with one hand at the maintenance man. "I suggest you get out."

The man didn't have to be told twice. He scurried away, still carrying the doorknob. LBJ came inside alone, pushed the door closed, then grimaced as it popped back open. He grabbed a chair and set it in front of the door, then glared at Kennedy.

The glare was effective in that hang-dog face, despite LBJ's attire. He wore a plaid silk pajama top stuffed into a pair of suitpants, finished with dress shoes and no socks. His hair—what remained of it—hadn't been Brilcremed down like usual, and stood up on the sides and the back.

"I get a phone call from some weasel underling of that Old Cocksucker, informing me that he's dead, and you're stealing from his tomb. I try to contact you, find out that you are indeed removing files from the Director's office, and that you won't take my calls. Now, I should've sent one of my boys over here, but I figured they're still walking on tip-toe around you because you're in fucking mourning, and this don't require tip-toe. Especially since you got to be wondering about now what the hell you did to deserve all of this."

"Deserve what?" Kennedy had expected LBJ's anger, but he hadn't expected it so soon. He also hadn't expected it here, in his office, instead of in the Oval Office a day or so later.

"Well, there's only two things that tie J. Edgar and your brother. The first is that someone was gunning for them and succeeded. The second is that they went after the mob on your bidding. There's a lot of shit running around here that says your brother's shooting was a mob hit, and I know personally that J. Edgar was doing his best to make it seem like that Oswald character acted alone. But now Edgar is dead and Jack is dead and the only tie they have is the way they kow-towed to your stupid prosecution of the men that got your brother elected."

Kennedy felt lightheaded. He hadn't even thought that the deaths of his brother and J. Edgar were connected. But LBJ had a point. Maybe there was a conspiracy to kill government officials. Maybe the mob was showing its power. He'd had warning.

Hell, he'd had suspicions. He hadn't let himself look at any of the evidence in his brother's assassination, not after he secured the body and prevented a disastrous autopsy in Texas. If those doctors at Parkland had done their job, they would've seen just how advanced Jack's Addison's disease was. The best kept secret of the Kennedy Administration—an administration full of secrets—was how close Jack was to incapacitation and death.

Kennedy clutched the file box. But LBJ knew that. He knew a lot of the secrets—had even promised to keep a few of them. And he wanted the files as badly as Kennedy did.

There had to be a lot in here on LBJ too. Not just the women, which was something he had in common with Jack, but other things, from his days in Congress.

"From what I heard," Kennedy said, making certain his voice was calm even though he wasn't, "all they know is someone shot Hoover. Did you get more details than that? Something that mentions organized crime in particular?"

"I'm sure it'll come out," LBJ said.

"You're sure that saying such things would upset me," Kennedy said. "You're after the files."

"Damn straight," LBJ said. "I'm the head of this government. Those files are mine."

"You're the head of this government for another year. Next January, someone'll take the oath of office and it might not be you. Do you really want to claim these in the name of the presidency? Because you might be handing them over to Goldwater come January."

LBJ blanched.

Someone knocked on the door, and startled both men. Kennedy frowned. He couldn't think of anyone who would have enough nerve to interrupt him when he was getting shouted at by LBJ. But someone had.

LBJ pulled the door open. Helen Gandy stood there.

"You boys can be heard in the hallway," she said, sweeping in as if the leader of the free world wasn't holding the door for her. "And it's embarrassing. It was precisely this kind of thing the Director hoped to avoid."

Then she nodded at LBJ. Kennedy watched her. The dragon lady. Jack, as usual, had been right with his jibes. Only the dragon lady would walk in here as if she were the most important person in the room.

"Mr. President," she said, "these files are the Director's personal business. He wanted me to take care of them, and get them out of the office, where they do not belong."

"Personal files, Miss Gandy?" LBJ asked. "These are his secret files."

"If they were secret, Mr. President, then you wouldn't be here. Mr. Hoover kept his secrets."

Mr. Hoover used his secrets, Kennedy thought, but didn't say.

"These are just his confidential files," Miss Gandy was

saying. "Let me take care of them and they won't be here to tempt anyone. That's what the Director wanted."

"These are government property," LBJ said with a sly look at Kennedy. For the first time, Kennedy realized his Goldwater argument had gotten through. "They belong here. I do thank you for your time and concern, though, ma'am."

Then he gave her a courtly little bow, put his hand on the small of her back, and propelled her out of the room.

Despite himself Kennedy was impressed. He'd never seen anyone handle the dragon lady that efficiently before.

LBJ grabbed one of the cabinets and slid it in front of the door he had just closed. Kennedy had forgotten how strong the man was. He had invited Kennedy down to his Texas ranch before the election, trying to find out what Kennedy was made of, and instead, Kennedy had realized just what LBJ was made of—strength, not bluster, brains *and* brawn.

He'd do well to remember that.

"All right," LBJ said as he turned around. "Here's what I'm gonna offer. You can have your family's files. You can watch while we search for them and you can have everything. Just give me the rest."

Kennedy raised his eyebrows. He hadn't felt this alive since November. "No."

"I can fire your ass in five minutes, put someone else in

this fancy office, and then you can't do a goddamn thing," LBJ said. "I'm being kind."

"There's historical precedent for a cabinet member barricading himself in his office after he got fired," Kennedy said. "Seems to me it happened to a previous president named Johnson. While I'm barricaded in, I'll just go through the files and find out everything I need to know."

LBJ crossed his arms.

It was a stand-off and neither of them had a good play. They only had a guess as to what was in those files—not just theirs but all of the others as well. They did know that whatever was in those files had given Hoover enough power to last in the office for more than forty years.

The files had brought down presidents. They could bring down congressmen, supreme court justices, and maybe even the current president. In that way, Helen Gandy was right.

The best solution was to destroy everything.

Only Kennedy wouldn't. Just like he knew LBJ wouldn't. There was too much history here, too much knowledge.

And too much power.

"These are our files," Kennedy said after a moment, although the word "our" galled him, "yours and mine. Right now we control them."

LBJ nodded, almost imperceptibly. "What do you want?"

What did he want? To be left alone? To have his family left alone? At midnight, he might have said that. But now, his old self was reasserting itself. He felt like the man who had gone after the corrupt leaders of the Teamsters, not the man who had accidentally gotten his brother murdered.

Besides, there might be things in that file that could head off other problems in the future. Other murders. Other manipulations.

He needed a bullet-proof position. LBJ was right: the Attorney General could be fired. But there was one position, constitutionally, that the president couldn't touch.

"I want to be your Vice President," Kennedy said. "And in 1972, when you can't run again, I want your endorsement. I want you to back me for the nomination."

LBJ swallowed hard. Color suffused his face and for a moment, Kennedy thought he was going to shout again.

But he didn't.

Instead he said, "And what happens if we don't win?"

"We move these to a location of our choosing. And we do it with trusted associates. We get this stuff out of here."

LBJ glanced at the door. He was clearly thinking of what Helen Gandy had said, how it was better to be rid of all of this than it was to have it corrupting the office, endangering everyone.

But if LBJ and Kennedy controlled the entire cache, they

also controlled their own files. LBJ could destroy his and Kennedy could preserve his family's legacy.

If it weren't for the fact that LBJ hated him almost as much as Kennedy hated LBJ, the decision would be easy.

"You'd trust me to a gentleman's agreement?" LBJ asked, not disguising the sarcasm in his tone. He knew Kennedy thought he was too uncouth to ever be considered a gentleman.

"You know where your interests lie. Just like I do," Kennedy said. "If we don't let Miss Gandy have the files, then this is the only choice."

LBJ sighed. "I hoped to be rid of the Kennedys by inauguration day."

"And what if I planned to run against you?" Kennedy asked, even though he knew he wouldn't. Already the party stalwarts had been approaching him about a 1964 presidential bid, and he had put them off. He had been too shaky, too emotionally fragile.

He didn't feel fragile now.

LBJ didn't answer that question. Instead, he said, "You can be an incautious asshole. Why should I trust you?"

"Because I saved Jack's ass more times than you can count," Kennedy said. "I'm saving yours too."

"How do you figure?" LBJ asked.

"Your fear of those files brought you to me, Mr. President." Kennedy put an emphasis on the title, which he usually avoided using around LBJ. "If I barricade myself in here, I'll have the keys to the kingdom and no qualms about letting the information free when I go free. If you work with me, your secrets remain just secrets."

"You're a son of bitch, you know that?" LBJ asked.

Kennedy nodded. "The hell of it is you are too or you wouldn't've brought up Jack's death before we knew what really happened to Hoover. So let's control the presidency for the next sixteen years. By then the information in these files will probably be worthless."

LBJ stared at him. It took Kennedy a minute to realize that although he'd won the argument, he wouldn't get an agreement from LBJ, not if Kennedy didn't make the first move.

Kennedy held out his hand. "Deal?"

LBJ stared at Kennedy's extended hand for a long moment before taking it in his own big clammy one.

"You goddamn son of a bitch," LBJ said. "You've got a deal."

———

I t took Bryce only one phone call. The guy who ran the motorpool told him who checked out the sedan without asking why Bryce want to know. And Bryce, as he leaned in the cold telephone booth half a block from the first crime scene, instantly understood what had happened and why.

The agent who checked out the sedan was Walter Cain. He should've been on extended leave. Bryce had recommended it after he had told Cain that his ex-fiancé had tried to commit suicide. On getting the news, Cain had just had that look, that blank, my-life-is-over look.

And it had scared Bryce. Scared him enough that he asked Cain be put on indefinite leave. How long ago had that been? Less than twelve hours.

More than enough time to get rid of the morals police —the one man who made all the rules at the FBI. The man who had no morals himself.

J. Edgar Hoover.

Bryce had spent the past week studying Cain's file. Cain had had HooverWatch off and on throughout the past year. Cain knew the procedure, and he knew how to thwart it.

He'd killed five agents.

Because no one would listen to Bryce about that vacant look in Cain's eye.

Bryce let himself out of the phone booth. He walked back to the coroner's van. If he didn't have back up by now, he'd call for some all over again. They couldn't leave him hanging on this. They had to let him know, if nothing else, what to do with the Director's body.

But he needn't've worried. When he got back to the alley, he saw five more sedans, all FBI issue. And as he stepped into the alley proper, the first person he saw was his boss, crouching over Hoover's corpse.

"I thought I told you to secure the scene," said the SAC for the District of New York, Eugene Hart. "In fact, I ordered you to do it."

"The scene extends over six blocks. I'm just one guy," Bryce said.

Hart walked over to him. He looked tired.

"I need to speak to you," Bryce said. He walked Hart back to the two sedans, explained what he'd learned, and watched Hart's face.

The man flinched, then, to Bryce's surprise, put his hand on Bryce's shoulder. "It's good work."

Bryce didn't thank him. He was worried that Hart hadn't asked any questions. "I'd heard Cain bitch more than once about Hoover setting the moral values for the office. And with what happened this week—"

"I know." Hart squeezed his shoulder. "We'll take care of it."

Bryce turned so quickly that he made Hart lose his grip. "You're going to cover it up."

Hart closed his eyes.

"You weren't hanging me out to dry. You were trying to figure out how to handle this. Son of a bitch. And you're going to let Cain walk."

"He won't walk," Hart said. "He'll just...be guilty of something else."

"You can't cover this up. It's too important. So soon after President Kennedy—"

"That's precisely why we're going to handle it," Hart said. "We don't want a panic."

"And you don't want anyone to know where Hoover and Tolson were found. What're you going to say? That they died of natural causes in their beds? Their *separate* beds?"

"It's not your concern," Hart said. "You've done well for us. You'll be rewarded."

"If I keep my mouth shut."

Hart sighed. He didn't seem to have the energy to glare. "I don't honestly care. I'm glad to have the old man gone. But I'm not in charge of this. We've got orders now, and everything'll get taken care of at a much higher level than either you or me.

You should be grateful for that."

Bryce supposed he should be. It took the political pressure off him. It also took the personal pressure off.

But he couldn't help feeling if someone had listened to him before, if someone had paid attention, then none of this would have happened.

No one cared that an FBI agent was going to marry a former prostitute. If the Bureau knew—and it did, then not even the KGB could use that as blackmail.

It was all about appearances. It would always be about appearances. Hoover had designed a damn booklet about appearances, and it hadn't stopped him from getting shot in a back alley after a party he would never admit attending.

Hoover had been so worried about people using secrets against each other, he hadn't even realized how his own secrets could be used against him.

Bryce looked at Hart. They were both tired. It had been a long night. And it would be an even longer few weeks for Hart. Bryce would get some don't-tell promotion and he'd stay there for as long as he had to. He had to make sure that Cain got prosecuted for something, that he paid for five deaths.

Then Bryce would resign.

He didn't need the Bureau, any more than he had needed Mary, his own pre-approved wife. Maybe he'd talk to O'Reilly, see if he could put in a good word with the NYPD. At least the NYPD occasionally investigated cases.

If they happened in the right neighborhood.

To the right people.

Bryce shoved his hands in his pockets and walked back to his apartment. Hart didn't try to stop him. They both knew Bryce's work on this case was done. He wouldn't even have to write a report.

In fact, he didn't dare write a report, didn't dare put any of this on paper where someone else might discover it. The wrong someone. Someone who didn't care about handling and the proper information.

Someone who would use that information to his own benefit.

Like the Director had.

For more than forty-five years.

Bryce shook the thought off. It wasn't his concern. He no longer had concerns. Except getting a good night's sleep.

And somehow he knew that he wouldn't get one of those for a long, long time.

YOU MIGHT LIKE THIS...
THE END OF THE WORLD

THEN

The air reeked of smoke.

The people ran, and the others chased them.

She kept tripping. Momma pulled her forward, but Momma's hand was slippery. Her hand slid out, and she fell, sprawling on the wooden sidewalk.

Momma reached for her, but the crowd swept Momma forward.

All she saw was Momma's face, panicked, her hands, grasping, and then Momma was gone.

Everyone ran around her, over her, on her. She put her hands over her head and cringed, curling herself into a little ball.

She made herself change color. Brown-gray like the sidewalk, with black lines running up and down.

Dress hems skimmed over her. Boots brushed her. Heels pinched the skin on her arms.

No spikes, Momma always said. *No spikes or they'll know.*

So she held her breath, hoping the spikes wouldn't break through her skin because she was so scared, and her side hurt where someone's boot hit it, and the wooden sidewalk bounced as more and more people ran past her.

Finally, she started squinching, like Daddy taught her before he left.

Slide, he said. *A little bit at a time. Slide. Squinch onto whatever surface you're on and cling.*

It was hard to squinch without spikes, but she did, her head tucked in her belly, her hair trailing to one side. More boots stomped on it, pulling it, but she bit her lower lip so that she wouldn't have to think about the pain.

She was almost to the bank door when the sidewalk stopped shaking. No one ran by her. She was alone.

She flattened herself against the brick and shuddered. Her skin smelled of chewing tobacco, spit and beer from the saloon next door.

She had shut down her ears, but she finally rotated them outward. Men were shouting, women yelling. There was pounding and screaming and a high-pitched noise she didn't like.

If they found her flattened against the brick, they'd know. If they saw the spikes rise from her body, they'd know. If they saw her squinching, they'd know.

But she couldn't move.

She was shivering, and she didn't know what to do.

NOW

The call didn't come through channels. It rang to Becca Keller's personal cell.

Chase Waterston hadn't even said hello.

"Got a problem at the End of the World," he'd said, his usually self-assured voice shaky. "Can you get here right away? Just you."

Normally, she would have told him to call the precinct or 911, but something stopped her. Probably that scared edge to his voice, a sound she'd never heard in all the years she'd known him.

She drove from the center of downtown Hope to the End of the World, a drive that, in the old days, would have taken five minutes. Now it took twenty, and the only thing that kept her from being annoyed at the traffic were the

73

mountains, bleak and cold, rising up like goddesses at the edge of Hope.

Hope was a mountain city, but its terrain was high desert. Vast expanses of brown still marked the outskirts of town, although the interior had lost much of its desert feel. By the time she passed the latest ticky-tacky development, she hit the rolling dunes of her childhood. Even though she had on the air-conditioning, the smell of sagebrush blew in —full of promise.

If she kept going straight too much farther, she'd hit small windy roads filled with switchbacks that led to now-trendy ski resorts. If she turned right, she'd follow the old stage coach route over the edge of the mountains into the Willamette Valley where most of Oregon's population lived.

The End of the World was an ancient resort at the fork between the mountain roads and the old stagecoach route. At the turn of the previous century, some enterprising entrepreneur figured travelers who were taking the narrow road toward the Willamette Valley would welcome a place to rest and recover from the long dusty trip.

Now bumper-to-bumper traffic filled that wagon route, which had expanded to a four-lane highway. Hope actually had a real rush hour, thanks to ex-patriate Californians, retired baby boomers, and ridiculously cheap housing.

Chase was rebuilding the resort for those baby boomers and Californians. For some reason, he thought they'd want to stay in a hundred-year-old hotel, with a view of the mountains and the river, even in the heat of the summer and the deep cold of the desert winter.

Becca steered the squad with her left hand and fiddled with the air-conditioner with her right, wishing her own car was out of the shop. No matter what she did, she couldn't get the squad car cooled. Nothing seemed to be working properly. Or maybe that was the effect of the heat.

It was a hundred and three degrees, and the third week without rain. The radio's most recent weather report promised the temperature would reach one hundred and eight by the time the day was over.

Finally, she reached the construction site.

Chase had set up the site so that it only blocked part of the ever-present wind and as a consequence, the dust billowed across the highway with the gusts.

The city had cited Chase twice for the hazard, and he'd promised to fix it just after the Fourth of July holiday. It looked like he'd been keeping his word, too. A huge plastic construction fence leaned against the old building. Graders and post-diggers were parked on the side of the road.

Nothing moved. Not the cats Chase had been using to dig out the old parking lot, not the crane he'd rented the week before, and not the crew, most of whom sat on the backs of pick-up trucks, their faces blackened with dust and grime and too much sun. She could see their eyes, white against the darkness of their skins, watching her as she turned onto the dirt path that Chase had been using as an access road.

He was waiting for her in the doorway of what had once been a natatorium. Built over an old underground spring, the Natatorium had once boasted the largest swimming pool in Eastern Oregon. There was some kind of pipe system which pumped water into the pool, keeping it perpetually cold. In the Natatorium's heyday, the water had been replaced daily.

Behind the Natatorium was the old five-story brick hotel that still had the original fixtures. No vandals had ever attacked the place. Even the windows were intact.

Becca had gone inside more than once, first as an impressionable twelve-year-old, and ever since, part of her believed the rumors that the hotel was haunted.

She pulled up beside the Natatorium door, in a tiny patch of shade provided by the overhanging roof. She got out and the blast-furnace heat hit her, prickling sweat on her skin almost instantly. Apparently the air conditioner had been working in the piece-of-crap squad after all.

Chase watched her. His lips were chapped, his skin fried blackish red from the sun. He had weather-wrinkles around his eyes and narrow mouth. His hair was cropped short, and over it he wore a regulation hardhat. He clutched another one in his left hand, slapping it rhythmically against his thigh.

"Thanks for coming, Becca," he said, and he still sounded shaken.

The tone was unfamiliar, but the expression on his face wasn't. She'd seen it only once, after she'd told him she wanted out, that his values and hers were so different, she couldn't stomach a relationship any longer.

"What do you got, Chase?" she asked.

"Come with me." He handed her the hardhat he'd been holding.

She took it as a gust of wind caught her short hair and blew its clipped edges into her face. She slipped the hardhat on, and tucked her hair underneath it, then followed Chase inside the building.

It was hotter inside the Natatorium, and the air smelled of rot and mold. She usually thought of those as humidity smells, but the Natatorium's interior was so dry that it was crumbly.

The floor was shredded with age, the wood so brittle that she wondered if it would hold her weight. Most of the walls were gone, the remains of them piled in a corner. Chase had gutted the interior.

When she had been a girl, she had played in this place. Her parents had forbidden her to come, which made it all the more inviting. The rot and mold smells had been present even then. But the walls had still been up, and there had been some ancient furniture in here as well, made unusable by weather and critters chewing the interior.

She used to stand inside the entrance with the door open, the stream of sunlight carrying a spinning tunnel of dust motes. When she closed her eyes halfway, she could just imagine the people arriving here after a long day of travel, happy to be in a place of such elegance, such warmth.

But now even that sense of a long ago but lively past was gone, and all that remained was the shell of the building itself—a hazard, an eyesore, something to be torn down and replaced.

Chase's boots echoed on the wood floor. He led her along the edges, pointing at holes closer to the center. She wondered if any of his employees had caused the holes, walking imprudently across the floor, foot catching on the weak spot, and then slipping through.

He was taking her to the employees' staircase in the back. When they reached it, she saw why. It was made of metal. Rusted metal, but metal all the same. Someone had recently bolted the stairs into the wall, probably under Chase's orders. A metal hand railing had been reinforced as well.

Chase looked over his shoulder to make sure she was following. She caught a glimpse of something in his face—reluctance? Fear? She couldn't quite tell—and then, as suddenly as it appeared, it was gone.

He went down the steps two at a time. She followed. Even though the handrail had been rebolted, the metal still flaked under her hand. The bolts might hold if she suddenly fell through the stairs but she wasn't sure if the railing would.

The smell grew stronger here, as if the mold had somehow managed to survive the dry summers. The farther down she went, the cooler the air got. It was still hot, but no longer oppressive.

Chase stopped at the bottom of the stairs. He watched her come down the last few, his gaze holding hers. The intensity of his gaze startled her. It was vulnerable, in a way she hadn't seen since their first year together.

Then he stepped away so that she could stand on the floor below.

The smell was so strong that it overwhelmed her. Beneath the mold and rot, there was something else, something familiar, something foul. It made the hair rise on the back of her neck.

"That way," Chase said, and this time she wasn't mistaking it. His voice was shaking. "I'll wait here."

She frowned at him, and then kept going. The floor here was covered in ceramic tile, chipped and broken, but sturdy. She wondered what was beneath it. Ground? Old-fashioned concrete? Wood? She couldn't tell. But the floor didn't creak here, and it felt solid.

A long wall hid everything from view. A door stood

open, sending in sunlight filled with dust motes, just like she remembered. Only there shouldn't be sunlight here. This was the basement, the miraculous swimming pool, the place that had helped make the End of the World famous.

She stepped through the door.

The light came from the back wall—or what had been the back. Chase's crew had destroyed this part of the building.

The basement of the End of the World was open to the air for the first time since it had been completed.

That strange feeling she'd had since she reached the bottom of the stairs grew. If the basement wasn't sealed, then the stench shouldn't have been so strong. The old air should have escaped, letting the freshness of the desert inside.

Some of the heat had trickled in, but not enough to dissipate the natural coolness. She stepped forward. The tile on the other side of the pool was hidden under mounds of dirt. The pool itself was half destroyed, but the cat which had done the damage wasn't anywhere near it. She could see the big tire tracks, scored deeply into the sandy earth, as if the cat itself had been stuck or if the operator had tried to escape in a hurry.

They had uncovered something. That much was clear. And she was beginning to get an idea as to what it was.

A body.

Given the smell, it had to have died here recently. Bodies didn't decay in the desert—not in the dry air and the sand. Inside a building like this, there might be standard decomposition, but considering how hot it had been, even that seemed unlikely.

She'd have to assume cause of death was suspicious because the body had been located here. And then she'd have to figure out a way to find out whose body it was.

She was already planning how she'd conduct her case when she stepped off the tile onto a mound of dirt, and peered into the gaping hole, and saw—

Bones. Piles of bones. Recognizable bones. Femurs, hip bones, pelvic bones, rib cages. Hundreds of human bones. And more skulls than she could count.

She rocked back on her heels, pressing her free hand to her face, the smell—the illogical and impossible smell— now turning her stomach.

A mass grave, of the kind she'd only seen in film or police academy photos.

A mass grave, anywhere from a hundred to seventy-five years old.

A mass grave, in Hope. She hadn't even heard rumors of it, and she had lived here all her life.

"Son of a bitch," she said.

"Yeah," Chase said from the stairs, "I couldn't agree more."

THEN

The screaming sent ripples through her. She couldn't complete the change. She couldn't even assume the color and texture of the brick.

Tears pricked her eyes. Tears, as big a giveaway as her hair, her fingers, her ears. Somehow, when she stopped the spikes, she stopped all her abilities.

Or maybe it was just the fear.

A door squeaked open, then boots hit the sidewalk. Polished boots with only a layer of black dust along the edge. Men's boots, not the dainty things Momma tried to wear.

She tried to will the shivering away, but she couldn't.

She couldn't move at all.

Not that she had anywhere to go.

She could only pray that he wouldn't look down, that he wouldn't see her, that she would be safe for just a little longer.

NOW

ecca stared at the hole. She couldn't even count all the skulls, rising like white stones out of the dirt. Not to mention the rib cages off to one side or the tiny bones lying in a corner, bones that probably belonged in a hand or a foot.

She couldn't do much on her own. But she could find out where that stink was coming from.

She turned around and headed for the stairs.

Chase tipped his hardhat back, revealing his dark eyes. "Where're you going?"

"To get some things from my evidence bag," Becca said.

"You're not going to call anyone, are you?" he asked.

She stopped in front of him. "I can't take care of this alone. You should know that."

He leaned against the railing, that assumed casual gesture which meant he was the most distressed. "This'll ruin me, Becca. Half my capital is in this place."

"You told me no good businessman ever invests his own money," she snapped, mostly because she was surprised.

He shrugged. "Guess I'm not a good businessman."

But he was. He had restored three of the downtown's oldest buildings, making them into expensive condominiums with views of the mountains. Single-handedly, he'd revitalized Hope's downtown, by adding trendy stores that the locals claimed would never succeed (yet somehow they did, thanks to the "foreigners," as the Californians were called) and restaurants so upscale that Becca would have to spend half a week's pay just to eat lunch.

"You knew I'd go by the book when you called me here," she said, more sharply than she intended. He'd gotten to her. That was the problem; he always did.

"I thought maybe we could talk. They're old bones. If we can get someone to recover them and keep it quiet—"

"How many workers saw this?" she asked. "Do you think they'll keep it quiet?"

"If I pay them enough," he said. "And if we move the bones to a proper cemetery."

"Is that what you think this is?" she asked. "A graveyard?"

"Isn't it?" He seemed genuinely surprised. "It was so far out in the desert when this place was built that it's possible—no, it's probable—that the memory of the graveyard got lost."

"I saw at least two ribcages with shattered bones, and several skulls looked crushed."

His lips trembled, and it was a moment before he spoke. "The equipment could have done that."

But he didn't sound convinced.

"It could have," she said. "But we need to know."

"Why?" he asked.

She looked over her shoulder. That patch of sunlight still glinted through the hole in the wall. The dust motes still floated. If she didn't look down, the place would seem just as beautiful and interesting as it always had.

"Because someone loved them once. Someone probably wants to know what happened to them."

"Someone?" He snorted. "Becca, the pool was put over a tennis court that was built at the turn of the 20th century. No one remembers these people. Only historians would care."

He paused, and she felt her breath catch.

Then he said, "This is my life."

He used a tone and inflection she used to find particularly mesmerizing. Once she told their couples therapist that with that tone, he could convince her to do anything, and that was when the therapist told her that she had to get out.

"It's a crime scene," Becca said, knowing that the argument was weak.

"You don't know that for sure, and even if it is, it's a hundred years old," he said.

"Then what's the smell?"

He frowned, clearly not understanding her.

"This is a desert, Chase. Bodies buried in dirt in a dry climate don't decay. They mummify."

He blinked. He obviously hadn't thought of that.

"And," she said, "even if they had decayed because of some strange environmental reason particular to this basement, they wouldn't smell after a hundred years."

That guarded expression had returned to his face. Only his eyes moved now.

"Maybe it's something small," he said. "A mouse, someone's lost cat."

She shook her head. "Smell's too strong, and over the entire building. If it were something small, the smell would have faded back when you broke open that wall."

"Not when it was dug up?" he asked, seeming surprised.

"No," she said. "Is that when you first smelled it?"

"That's when they called me."

They, meaning his crew. She frowned at him, wondering if he was going to blame them.

But for what? A smell?

She'd have to find the source before she made assumptions.

And that, she knew, was going to be hard.

THEN

A hand touched her shoulder. A human hand, warm and gentle. Another shivery ripple ran through her. She still had a shoulder; she hadn't gotten rid of that either. How silly she must look, plastered against the brick wall like a half formed younglin.

Screams still echoed. The shouts had died down, although sometimes they rose up altogether, like a group got excited about something.

"You're one of them, aren't you?"

Male voice, human, just as gentle as the hand. She couldn't stop shivering.

"I won't hurt you."

She resisted the urge to rotate an eye upwards, so that she could see more than the boot.

"But you better come with me before they find you."

That did startle her. Her eye moved before she could stop it. It formed above her shoulder. He jumped back slightly when her eye appeared, but his hand never left her skin, even though it was finally turning tannish-red like the brick.

She'd seen him before. Daddy had laughed with him in the good days. He had slicked-back hair and a narrow face and kind eyes.

He crouched beside her, and looked right at her eye, like it didn't bother him, even though she knew it did. He wouldn't've jumped like that if it didn't.

"Please," he said, "come with me. I don't know when they're coming back. And someone might see us. Please."

She had to form a mouth. Her nose remained, tucked against her stomach from when she'd formed a ball, but her mouth had disappeared when she had tried to take on the appearance of the wooden sidewalk.

It took all her strength to make the mouth come out near the eye, and from the look of disgust that passed over his face, she still didn't look right. Her hair was on the other side of her body, and her eye was just above her shoulder. The mouth had probably come out on what would have been her back if she put herself together right.

Right being human.

That's what Momma said.

Momma.

"Please," he said again, and this time, she heard panic in his voice.

"Stuck," she said.

"Oh, Christ." He looked up and down the street, then at the buildings across from it.

He seemed younger than she remembered, or maybe she was as bad at telling human ages as Momma was.

"How do we get you unstuck?" he asked.

She didn't know. She'd never been like this, not this scared, not all by herself.

She tried to shrug and felt her other shoulder form into the wood. A splinter dug into her skin, and her entire body turned red with pain.

"What a mess," he said, and she didn't know if he meant her or what was going on or how scared they both seemed to be.

She willed herself to let go, but she was attached to the brick, and she'd lost control of half her body functions. Daddy said fear would do that.

Whatever happens, baby, he'd say, *you have to trust us. You have to believe we'll get together again. Let that be your strength, so that you never, ever succumb to fear.*

But he'd been gone for a long time now. And Momma hadn't come back for her, even though people were screaming.

The man tried to pry a flat corner of her skin from the edge of the brick. She could feel the tug, saw his face scrunch up in disgust when he got to the sticky underneath part.

"How'd you get there?" he asked.

"Squinched," she said.

"Squinched." He didn't understand. And she spoke his language, she knew she did. She formed the right mouth, she'd been using the words for a long time now, and she knew how they felt inside her brain and out.

"Can you show me?" he asked. "Can you squinch onto my arm?"

She wasn't supposed to squinch to a human. Momma was strict about that. Like there was something bad about it, something awful would happen.

But something awful was happening now.

The screams...

"No," she said, even though that had to be a lie. Momma and Daddy wouldn't forbid something if she couldn't've done it in the first place.

"God," he said, then looked down the street where the screams had come from. Where the shouts had grown more and more angry every time they rose up.

Right now, it was quiet, and she hated that more.

She hated it all.

"Stay here," he said.

He stood up, letting go of her shoulder. The warm vanished, and the fear rose even worse. Her other shoulder disappeared, and she felt the spikes, threatening to appear.

She had to close both eyes and will the spikes away.

When she opened the eyes, he was gone.

She moved the eyes all over her skin, looking for him, and she didn't see him at all.

The street was still empty, and too quiet.

Then, faraway, someone laughed. A mean, nasty, brittle laugh.

She folded her ears inside her skin, and willed herself flat, hoping, this time, that it would work.

NOW

ecca climbed the stairs, clinging to the handrail, the rust flaking against her palms. She had to call for help. At most, she needed a coroner, and probably a few officers just to search for the source of that smell.

But she felt guilty about calling. Chase used to talk about restoring the End of the World when she'd met him. He had brought her out here on their first date, even though she'd told him that she had explored the property repeatedly when she was a child.

Maybe they'd be able to keep this out of the paper, particularly if it turned out to be a graveyard or a dumping ground. But even that probably wouldn't happen.

The newspapers seemed to love this kind of story.

If she reported this, she would condemn Chase's

project to a kind of limbo. With so much capital invested, he probably couldn't afford to wait until the legal issues were solved.

She almost turned around to ask him how much time he could give them, but then she'd be compromising the investigation. For all she knew, there was a recently killed human beneath that dirt, and someone (Chase?) was using the old bones to hide it.

Then she shook her head. Not Chase. He was manipulative and difficult, moody and untrustworthy, but he wasn't—nor had he ever been—violent.

She sighed and continued up the stairs. Much as she wanted to help him, she couldn't. She had an obligation to the entire community.

She had an obligation to herself.

The wind hit her the moment she stepped outside. Bits of sand stung her skin, sticking to the sweat. Even with the sun, it now felt cooler out here because of that wind.

The construction workers watched her. She didn't know most of them; the town had grown too big for her to know everyone by sight like she had when she was a child. Many of these workers were Hispanic, some of them probably illegal.

Hispanics expected her to check their papers. She was supposed to do that too, although she never did. She didn't object to people who worked hard and tried to improve their lives.

With one hand, she tipped her hardhat back and nodded toward the workers. Then she opened the squad's driver's door, and winced at the heat which poured out at her. She leaned inside, unwilling to go into that heat voluntarily, and grabbed the radio's handset.

She paused before turning it on, knowing that even that momentary hesitation was a victory for Chase.

Then she clicked the handset and asked the dispatch to send Jillian Mills.

Jillian Mills was the head coroner for Hope and the surrounding counties. She actually worked the job full time, but her assistants were dentists and veterinarians, and one retired doctor.

"You want the crime scene unit?" the dispatch asked. It was standard procedure for a crime scene unit to come with the coroner.

"Not yet," Becca said. "I'm not sure what exactly we have here, except that it's dead."

Which was technically true, if she ignored all the crushed and broken bones.

"Tell her to hurry," Becca added. "It's hot as hell out here and there's a construction crew waiting."

That usually worked to get any city official moving. Lately, the "foreigners" had taken to suing the city if their emergency or official personnel delayed money-making operations, even for a day.

Chase would never do that—he knew that getting

along with the city helped his permits go through and his iffy projects get approved—but Becca still used the excuse.

She didn't want to be here any longer than she had to.

She stood, lifted her hardhat, and wiped the sweat off her forehead. Then she closed the door and leaned on it for a moment.

The End of the World.

She wondered if Chase had ever thought that the name might have been prophetic.

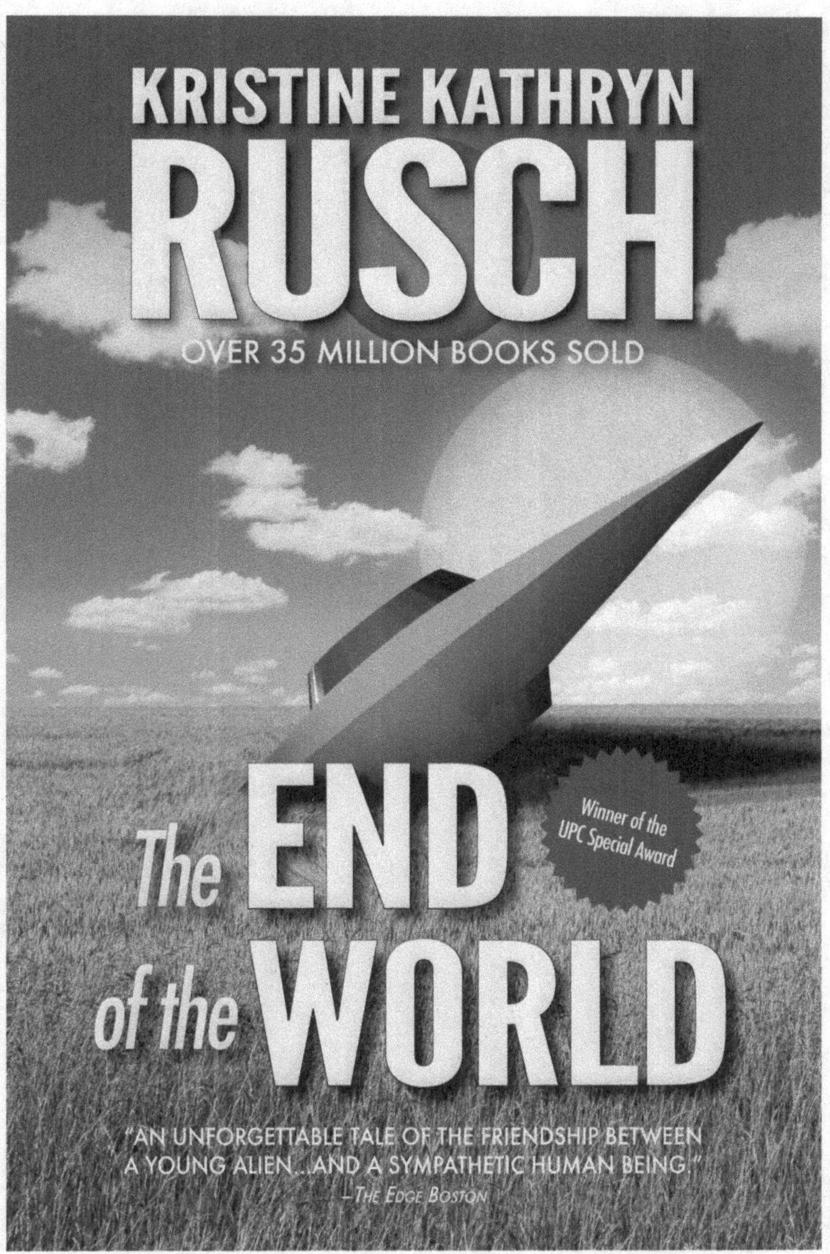

Keep Reading *The End of the World!*

Go to www.wmgbooks.com

HEAR DIRECTLY FROM KRIS

Sign up for the Kristine Kathryn Rusch newsletter and hear directly from Kris herself.

Go to kriswrites.com.

Get the latest news and releases from all of the WMG authors and lines, including Kristine Kathryn Rusch, Kristine Grayson, Kris Nelscott, Dean Wesley Smith, *Pulphouse Fiction Magazine, Smith's Monthly,* and so much more.

Go to wmgbooks.com.

You can also follow Kris on Bookbub.

We value honest feedback, and would love to hear your opinion in a review, if you're so inclined, on your favorite book retailer's site.

ABOUT THE AUTHOR

New York Times bestselling author Kristine Kathryn Rusch writes in almost every genre. Her novels have made bestseller lists around the world and her short fiction has appeared in eighteen best of the year collections. She has won more than twenty-five awards for her fiction, including the Hugo, Le Prix Imaginales, the Asimov's Readers Choice award, and the Ellery Queen Mystery Magazine Readers Choice Award.

Rusch writes in many genres, from science fiction to mystery, from western to romance. She has written under a pile of pen names, but most of her work appears as Kristine Kathryn Rusch. Her Kris Nelscott pen name has won or been nominated for most of the awards in the mystery genre, and her Kristine Grayson pen name became a bestseller in romance. Her science fiction novels set in the bestselling Diving Universe have won dozens of awards and are in development for a major TV show. She also writes the Retrieval Artist sf series and several major series that mostly appear as short fiction.

Rusch broke a number of barriers in the sf/f field, including being the first female editor of *The Magazine of Fantasy & Science Fiction*. She has owned two different publishing companies, and writes a highly regarded publishing industry blog on Patreon. She also writes a highly regarded weekly publishing industry blog. Find out more about her work at kriswrites.com, and more on all her books at wmgbooks.com.

facebook.com/kristinekathrynruschwriter
patreon.com/kristinekathrynrusch
bookbub.com/authors/kristine-kathryn-rusch

www.ingramcontent.com/pod-product-compliance
Lightning Source LLC
Chambersburg PA
CBHW010737100726
47899CB00009B/3095